UNFRIENDLY FIRE

I peeked around the building.

A car stopped near Jimmy. The shadows and trees made it hard to see. Four guys slouched low in the car. I could barely see their heads. I thought maybe they were asking Jimmy for directions.

Then gunshots exploded.

White angry fire flashed from the backseat.

Jimmy fell.

LYNNE EWING

DRIVE-BY

▄ HarperTrophy®
A Division of HarperCollinsPublishers

Harper Trophy® is a registered trademark of
HarperCollins Publishers Inc.

Library of Congress Cataloging-in-Publication Data
Ewing, Lynne
   Drive-by / Lynne Ewing.
      p.   cm.
      Summary: Twelve-year-old Tito, while helping to care for his little
sister, struggles to find his way during the aftermath of his brother's
death in a gang-related shooting.
   ISBN 0-06-027125-6. — ISBN 0-06-027126-4 (lib. bdg.)
   ISBN 0-06-440649-0 (pbk.)
   [1. Gangs—Fiction.   2. Death—Fiction.   3. Brothers and sisters—
Fiction.]   I. Title.
PZ7.E965Dr   1996   95-40643
[Fic]—dc20   CIP
                                                                AC

Typography by Alison Donalty
❖
First Harper Trophy edition, 1998

Visit us on the World Wide Web!
http://www.harperchildrens.com

11 12 13   LP/CW   30 29 28 27 26 25 24

For
Amber Fitzgerald,
Jonathan Fitzgerald, and
Mair Jack Mayesh

I don't go out at night anymore.

Sometimes I have to for Mom.

Like the night Jimmy died.

Jimmy was my brother. Mom laughed at all his dumb jokes. She called him funny bones.

I've never known anyone who could make people laugh as much as Jimmy could.

Mina, my little sister, giggled at Jimmy's faces. Mina wants to be a princess when she grows up. She's still at an age where she thinks that's possible.

I'm the serious one. Jimmy called me a worry toad.

That made Mom laugh.

They're all good-looking. Not me. I don't look like I belong in the same family. My nose is too big for my face. My eyes are too small for my nose. Mom says I have character, though. Zev across the street says that means I'm honest and dependable.

The night Jimmy died, Jimmy and I were walking Mina home from a birthday party. Mina had tied her long black hair on one side in a ponytail. She thinks that's what a princess does.

Near the library, the wind started blowing. Leaves fell from the elm trees and scattered across the sidewalk. The library, dark and silent, had been closed for a long time. It looked haunted. Everyone said it was.

So, of course, Jimmy decided to play the claw.

"I can't control my hand," he yelled.

He made his right hand into a claw.

"Help me," he cried.

Mina screamed.

"Don't do it, Jimmy," I said. "We're already late."

Jimmy stumbled around, fighting his right hand. He used to scare me with that claw routine, too.

He ran after Mina. He made it look like his hand was chasing Mina. He staggered after her, fighting his hand.

She squealed and ran.

I hated Jimmy's claw routine more than anything. There was no way you could stop him when he started.

That was the last thing I saw him do.

Mina ran behind the library.

"Great work, Clawman," I said. "We were supposed to be home an hour ago."

That was my fault mostly. I couldn't say no to a second piece of chocolate birthday cake.

"Don't be such a worry toad," Jimmy said. Then he smiled.

I shook my head. "We shouldn't be out this late."

"Tito, relax. Okay?" Jimmy said.

My real name is Timothy Thomas, but everyone calls me Tito.

I left Jimmy alone on the sidewalk and ran after Mina.

Behind the library, wind rushed through the trees, making shadows shift and change shape. Branches creaked and groaned.

I found Mina right away. Without the claw chasing her, she didn't think it was fun to run and scream. Besides, it was dark and scary behind the library.

"You got to stop running away from me," I said. "Someday I won't be able to find you."

She didn't answer. She didn't think a brother should talk to his princess sister that way.

We walked toward the front of the library, our shoes kicking up dead leaves.

That's when I heard music, hard and heavy loud music. The beat made my chest pound. I knew gangbangers were rolling nearby.

Tires skidded.

I peeked around the building.

A car stopped near Jimmy. The shadows and trees made it hard to see. Four guys slouched low in the car. I could barely see their heads. I thought maybe they were asking Jimmy for directions.

Then gunshots exploded.

White angry fire flashed from the backseat.

Mina grabbed her ears. When she feels really scared, she doesn't scream and run. She freezes and sucks in air in a long sigh.

Jimmy fell.

I knew he was teasing, and it made me angry. I couldn't believe he'd tease me that way.

I only thought that for a heartbeat.

The car sped away. The taillights—different

colors, one red, one orange—blurred as the car disappeared around the corner.

I ran to Jimmy.

I've never run as fast as I did that night.

I kept hoping he'd get up. I wanted him to laugh at me for being so scared and call me a pathetic worry toad.

Jimmy lay still as a stone. Something seeped onto the sidewalk around him.

I stopped and pushed Mina behind me.

"Go sit on the steps," I said.

"No," she said, and ran to Jimmy, her ponytail flying.

I didn't want her to see Jimmy like that.

I grabbed her and carried her to the library steps. She dug her face into my shoulder and sobbed. She had seen too much.

I went back and stood over Jimmy. I cried, too.

Things don't always make sense. Animals don't kill other animals for fun. So why do people kill each other? All Jimmy ever did was make people laugh.

When you're little and something like this happens, you always wake up. It's a nightmare and your mom is sitting on the edge of your bed. Now

I felt like someone had pushed me into a nightmare while I was wide awake.

Two police cars pulled up without sirens. The cars stopped near Jimmy. The headlights shone over him.

The cops walked quietly and whispered like ghosts. They were afraid gangbangers might hear and come check things out and then go kill someone else in revenge.

A huge man with hands bigger than basketballs came over and stood next to me.

"I'm Detective Howard," he said. "Do you know the boy who was killed?"

I nodded. "My brother."

"I'm sorry, son," he said, and squatted next to me.

He wrote down information about Jimmy and about me in a small notebook, all the time talking in a low, sad voice.

"I think the shooting might have been in revenge for a shooting last week a few blocks away," he said. "Do you know what gang Jimmy belonged to?"

"Jimmy was no gangbanger," I said.

Jimmy always told me there were only two

kinds of gangbangers: those who were dead and those who were going to die. Joining a gang didn't make sense to Jimmy, so I knew he wouldn't do it.

"Jimmy's been jacking people for their money and rolling with some dope-dealing killers," Detective Howard said.

"That's not true," I said. "Jimmy wasn't involved in the gang thing."

Jimmy was innocent. Everyone knows the guys doing the shooting want to kill gang members, but sometimes they settle for killing someone who lives in the gang's neighborhood.

"You know Lamar Callas or Ice Breaker Joe?"

"Everyone does," I said.

"Jimmy was their ace man."

"You're wrong," I said.

The detective patted my head. I jerked away. I didn't want a liar touching me.

"Can you identify the car?"

"It was too dark."

He handed me his card. "Call me if you think of anything."

The ambulance came.

Mina stayed on the steps and cried.

I thought I should go to her, but I couldn't leave

Jimmy. The ambulance attendants wrapped him in white cloth and put him in the ambulance.

"Be careful with him," I yelled. I don't think anyone heard me.

The ambulance doors slammed.

A fireman washed away the blood. I hadn't seen the fire truck until then.

Someone tapped my shoulder.

"I'll take you home," Detective Howard said.

I went to get Mina.

2

Three television cameras watched us at the funeral.

I could look over and see a reflection of myself in the camera lens. The last thing I wanted to see was the way my face looked at Jimmy's funeral.

The local TV stations were helping to raise money for Mom to pay for Jimmy's funeral. I guess they thought that gave them the right to be in our faces.

Mom wanted Jimmy to have a proper funeral. Roses and carnations filled the church and made the air too sweet to breathe. Strangers sent Jimmy flowers. Even some famous people did. I wish people had paid that kind of attention to him when he was alive. They would have liked Jimmy. Everyone did. He could make anyone laugh.

I watched Mom. I didn't think she'd ever smile again. I knew I wouldn't.

After the funeral neighbors came to our house. They brought Jell-O salads and cold fried chicken and tried to make Mom feel better.

Zev brought his chess set. He's always reading or playing chess. I don't think he had even thrown a baseball since his family came to the United States from Russia.

"You want to learn how to play chess?" he asked.

"No," I said.

Mom always tried to make me play with him.

I did once. Mumblety-peg. I got in trouble for playing with a jackknife. Then I got in trouble for making Zev pull the peg out of the ground with his teeth. That's what the loser has to do in mumblety-peg. Try to explain that to your mom.

Zev followed me into the kitchen. Casseroles and cakes lined the kitchen counter. I don't understand why people eat after funerals.

"Do you want something to eat?" Zev asked. "My mother says there's nothing better for a boy than that he should eat."

Zev's mom had brought over her baked-potato

pudding. Usually I can eat three helpings, but I didn't feel like eating without Jimmy calling me a sloppy pig.

I went outside.

Zev started to follow me.

I turned at the door.

"Zev, do you mind?" I asked.

"Mind what?" he said.

"I want to be alone."

"My mother said you would need a friend to talk to," Zev said.

I almost said, "Yeah, well I don't see Gus here," but I stopped. Zev didn't have any friends. He wasn't funny and cool like Gus. Zev looked like he believed what his mom said about nothing being better for a boy than eating. He weighed as much as Gus and me together.

"Not tonight," I said instead.

I went outside and sat on the swing near the garage.

Mina followed me outside and crawled on my lap.

That's when loud music came like thunder down the alley.

I didn't have to ask Mina if it sounded like the same music we heard the night Jimmy was killed.

She sucked in air in a long sigh and pinched my arm.

The music thumped my heart around inside my rib cage.

A blue Oldsmobile rolled slowly down the alley toward us. Tires crunched over rocks and gravel.

I hid Mina behind a bush; then I ducked inside the garage.

I peeked out the dusty window.

The car stopped.

I couldn't breathe, my chest hurt so badly. My leg jumped all over with nerves.

Lamar Callas sat in the passenger seat. Ice Breaker Joe drove the car.

The back car door opened. A guy wearing a baseball cap jumped out. He wore a bandanna over his face like a bandit.

He walked into the backyard. He reminded me of someone, but I couldn't think who.

All of a sudden, he ran back to the car. His back was to me, so I couldn't tell if he had something in his arms or not.

The tires grabbed the gravel and spun. The car sped away, throwing gravel all over the alley.

A spray of pebbles pinged the window in front of me.

I ran to tell Mina she could come out from behind the bush.

Mina was gone.

3

"Mina!"

I looked around the bushes, then on the other side of the garage and in the alley.

I ran down the side yard. Leaves and branches on the big hibiscus bush scraped my arms and face.

The front gate was locked. I didn't think Mina could unlock the gate by herself.

I looked up and down the street anyway.

"Mina!"

I ran to the backyard.

Mom came flying out the back door. The screen door pounded behind her.

"What happened?"

"Some guys came by and I hid Mina. Now I can't find her."

"Maybe she's in the alley," Mom said.

We both ran until our feet crunched the gravel in the alley.

Broken glass shone like silver and jewels in the moonlight.

I thought I saw Mina picking up a piece of glass. That would be just like her, collecting jewels when we're going crazy looking for her.

I ran that way. Mom ran behind me.

"Mina?"

A poinsettia bush bobbing in the wind made the shadow.

Mom put her hand on my shoulder. I wished she hadn't. I could feel her cold fingers trembling against my skin.

"Mina always wanders off," I said. "She does it all the time. You better talk to her."

People were coming out to the backyard.

"What's wrong?" Zev's mother asked. She always wore a head scarf and a long skirt.

"Go on home," I yelled. "All of you. Haven't you seen enough?"

"Tito," Mom said. "They just want to help."

Mom tried to put her arm around me. I jerked away and ran down the alley.

"Timothy Thomas!" Mom yelled after me.

I wanted to go back to her. I would have if the whole neighborhood hadn't been in our backyard.

When I got to the street, I looked both ways trying to think where Mina might have gone. She loves French fries more than anything. If she ever does become a princess, she'll eat French fries at Big Molly's Diner for every meal.

Maybe I could find her there.

That's when I heard feet pounding behind me.

Zev ran up to me, wheezing and trying to breathe.

"I'll help you look for Mina," he said.

I almost said yes. Zev looked so sad and lonely behind his glasses.

But then I turned and ran the six blocks to Big Molly's Diner.

Inside, the diner smelled of fried onions and hamburgers. I hadn't eaten since before the funeral, and the smells woke up my stomach.

I walked from one end of the diner to the other. I thought I'd find Mina sitting on one of the red stools.

I turned to leave when a man left his seat at the counter. He also left a big pile of fries on his plate.

I sat on his stool and salted the fries, then

looked around. No one noticed me. Jimmy taught me how to do this. People always waste food.

The manager came over. He's Big Molly's son, Sonny. He's tall and thin. Big Molly is tall and fat.

"Great fries," I said, and bit into another.

Sonny shook his head and set a clean glass of water in front of me.

"Thanks," I said.

Sonny walked away.

Jimmy said other people didn't like to see food go to waste either.

I watched the door. I figured Mina would pop in any minute.

The only person who popped in was Zev.

He sat down next to me at the counter.

He didn't say a word.

He couldn't.

He gasped and gulped for air like a big red whale.

Sonny came over and stood next to us.

"Son, you okay?" he asked.

Zev nodded.

"He's with me," I said.

Finally, Zev and I walked home. I hoped Mom had found Mina by now.

Mom stood on the front sidewalk with Mrs. Washington, our next-door neighbor. Mrs. Washington had her arm around Mom's shoulder. I knew right away they hadn't found Mina.

A police car stopped in front of the house.

I walked slower and slower. Zev's hot hand held my shoulder.

Detective Howard stepped from the car.

I couldn't breathe.

What happened to Mina?

4

A second policeman helped Mina from the back of the squad car.

"We found her at the funeral home," Detective Howard said. "She was looking for Jimmy."

Mom bit her lip. She picked up Mina and held her tightly.

Mina must have thought death was a place, like Boston or something, and Jimmy could come back for a visit. She was too young to understand that death was final.

That night, Mom told us we were safe.

"Everything's okay," she said.

But when she made a bed for Mina in the bathtub and told me to sleep on the floor, I knew she thought something more would happen.

Mina cried herself to sleep. The old metal bathtub echoed her crying. It sounded like a sad, lonely ghost was haunting our house.

I had never slept on the floor before except at sleepovers.

I hadn't slept alone before either. I hated the way Jimmy knocked around and kicked me in his sleep.

Now I missed it.

I fell asleep and dreamed about Jimmy.

He was running from me. Every time I ran close enough to tag him, he would take off again. Then he jumped into the back of an ambulance, and the ambulance doors slammed in my face.

I woke with a start and sat up.

At first I thought I had fallen out of bed; then I remembered I had gone to sleep on the floor.

I looked at the clock. It was three in the morning.

I could still hear Mina's crying. I stood and walked down the hall to comfort her.

Something was wrong.

I stopped. The crying came from another part of the house.

I tiptoed to the back of the house.

Mom sat at the kitchen table, crying. She held a picture of Jimmy in her hands.

"My poor funny bones," she said, and then she cried some more.

I went back to bed, shivering, and bit my pillow.

I didn't want to cry, because I knew it would make Jimmy sad if he could look down and see all of us crying.

I cried anyway.

5

Mom walked Mina to school.

The morning kindergarten starts twenty minutes before the other grades. Usually I walk Mina to school, but sometimes when Mom has the day off, she walks Mina to kindergarten. Then she comes home and talks to me for a few minutes before I leave. I like going to school early so I can hang out with my friends or work the computers.

After Mom and Mina left, I dug in the back of the closet for Jimmy's old tennis shoes and put them on. I knew Mom wouldn't want me to wear them. She'd say they were too big and would ruin my feet, or I'd fall and break an ankle.

I wore them anyway.

Someone knocked on the front door.

I knew it was pesky Zev.

I dodged out the back and ran down the alley. I

tried to feel what Jimmy's feet must have felt like in the shoes. He was a good runner.

At Mountain Street School, plywood covered most of the windows. Graffiti covered the plywood. The names don't make sense anymore. That doesn't stop anyone from spraying on his own tag.

Lots of schools in L.A. have metal detectors. Mountain Street School doesn't have one yet. I try not to think about it, but sometimes you hear about kids sneaking guns to school.

Mrs. Bilky stood in front of class showing us magnets. As if we hadn't seen that a million times before sixth grade.

Everyone was zoning out.

I stared at Lisa Tosca. She was the prettiest girl in school. I had never spoken to her. Yet. I liked to plan ways to meet her. Maybe I'd win an award and she would come up and congratulate me. Or maybe I'd crawl up a tree and save her cat, if she had one.

Gus Clayton sat in front of me in Mrs. Bilky's class. Gus was my best friend since first grade. He hadn't gone to Jimmy's funeral. I wanted him to. But I understood. He had problems of his own.

He turned to me.

"I'm going to run away," he said.

"Don't, Gus," I said.

I felt sorry for him. He had no one at home who cared enough about him to go looking for him if he did run away.

"Gus," Mrs. Bilky yelled at him, like he was the only kid in class not paying attention.

I wanted to stand up and tell her that enough people were yelling at Gus already.

"I was the one talking, Mrs. Bilky," I said.

"I see," she said, as if it made sense that I was talking because my brother had died.

She turned back to her magnets. I could hear the magnets clicking together on her desk.

"You're the fastest runner at school," I whispered to Gus. "Stay, and maybe if you keep running you can win an award or even go to the Olympics."

"I'm going to run," he said.

I knew he didn't mean track.

I didn't have time to worry about Gus. Things were changing too fast to think about anything but Mom and Mina and me.

I walked home by myself. I watched the street now. Passing cars made me nervous.

I had a strange feeling as I got close to the house.

The house looked different.

For one thing, all the shades were pulled. For another, I couldn't hear the TV. I should have been able to hear Nickelodeon. Mina was always watching it.

I decided to check the back of the house first.

I walked around to the alley, then climbed over the fence into Mrs. Washington's yard.

I know her dog, Spider. I think everyone does. His legs don't match his body. He looks as if he's walking on stilts. His body is round and his legs are spindly and long like a spider. That's how he got his name.

Spider wagged his tail. It's as long and as skinny as his legs. I guess he thought I was coming to play with him.

I stood on his doghouse.

Spider barked and tried to jump on top of his doghouse with me.

I looked over the fence.

I couldn't see anyone in the kitchen window. It was too dark inside to see anything, really.

Mom should have been making dinner. She always spends a long time cooking dinner. She's a great cook; even when it seems like there's no food in the house for dessert, she makes something. She can make candy from grapefruit peel and apple pie from crackers. Sometimes she makes candy with leftover mashed potatoes, powdered sugar, and peanut butter.

I climbed over the fence and walked slowly up to the back door.

I opened the door and walked inside.

The house was empty.

I stood in the kitchen for a long minute.

Even the refrigerator was gone. Little gray dust balls wiggled in a draft where the refrigerator had been.

I looked on the counter for a note, then peeked inside the living room. What I saw made my blood run cold.

Spray-paint graffiti covered the walls.

A crew of taggers had broken into the house and written on the living-room walls.

These guys write anywhere. One time I saw a guy shove his foot in the exhaust pipe on a bus. He jumped up and wrote his tag while the bus pulled away from the curb.

I took another step.

The floorboards creaked. I knew this house. I had lived here since I could remember. One thing

I knew, the floorboards didn't creak where I was walking.

The sound came from the back of the house. Someone was inside with me.

I crept from the living room to the hallway. All the time I prayed the other person in the house was Mom. I hoped she was packing my things. I wanted her to tell me what was going on.

Another part of me knew the other person could be some bandit tagger or a gangbanger.

I held my breath and hid in the first bedroom.

The room was empty except for a broken Christmas-tree light on the floor.

Floorboards creaked again.

Someone was coming toward me.

I pressed flat against the wall.

Then I heard loud music. The music hurt my ears and made the walls vibrate. I eased to the window and peeked outside.

A chopped black Chevrolet swerved against the curb.

Suddenly someone grabbed my shoulder and yanked me into the hallway, then dragged me into the kitchen, pulling me with a force I couldn't believe.

Next thing I knew, I was facedown in the dirt in the backyard as if I had lost at mumblety-peg.

That's when gunfire opened on the house.

8

I couldn't breathe. Someone was on top of me. I tried to scream, but grass and dirt filled my mouth. Mud packed into my nose.

Plaster and stucco flew around me.

Terrible explosions thundered in my ears; then the gunfire stopped.

Tires screeched.

It was silent for about two seconds before police cars skidded to a stop at the front curb. Police radios crackled in front of the house.

The weight lifted off me.

I turned.

Gus stood over me, brushing dirt off his jeans.

I spit out dirt and grass. Then I wiped my nose on my T-shirt.

"Man, you're a sorry case for staying alive in

this city," Gus said. "Don't you know they're after you?"

"Me?"

"'Cause of your brother, man," Gus said.

"Jimmy was no gangbanger," I said.

"Everyone in this town is ganging and banging," Gus said.

We heard steps inside the house, and then tires crunched gravel in the alley.

"Run!" Gus yelled.

"Why?" I asked.

"You don't know anything about surviving in this city."

He jerked my hand, and then I was flying over the fence with him, splinters sinking into my belly.

I fell near Spider. Spider growled and pounced at me.

I was dead for sure.

Spider jumped over my head and lunged at Gus.

Gus ran for the next fence and pulled himself up.

Spider bit his jeans and held tight. The dog yanked his head from side to side and growled.

The jeans slipped off. Gus fell behind the fence.

Spider brought the jeans to me as proud as if he had caught a cat.

I took the jeans and petted his head.

Someone looked over the fence into Mrs. Washington's yard. I could see the shadow on the lawn in front of me.

I hoped it was a cop but I wasn't going to test my luck and see. Maybe it was one of the guys in the black Chevrolet.

I hid inside the doghouse with the jeans.

Fleas thought I was dinner.

Spider pushed into the doghouse with me, his skinny feet poking my legs. His wagging tail hit my face.

I didn't know what to do. How would I know when it was safe? Would it ever be safe?

9

It felt like I was in that smelly doghouse with Spider breathing in my face for at least half an hour. Then someone called my name.

"Timothy Thomas Cahill, what are you doing in the doghouse?"

No one except Mom ever calls me Timothy Thomas, not unless I'm in a world of trouble.

I peeked out. I could hardly see, the way Spider licked my face like I was a giant human lollipop.

"You come in here right now." Mrs. Washington stood on the porch, her hands fisted on her wide hips. She wore a green robe, and pink curlers in her hair.

You don't argue with Mrs. Washington.

I started to the back door. Gus leaned over the fence with his hand reaching out. I tossed his jeans to him.

"Man, you're a sorry case for keeping your pants on in this city," I said, and smiled.

He smiled back, but then he made some kind of gang sign with his hand.

That made me sad.

I went inside. Our refrigerator sat on the back porch. I'd know that refrigerator anywhere. When I was three, I colored on it with a green marker. Mom never got all the color off.

In the kitchen Mom sat at the table with a cup of coffee. She had a wide-eyed look on her face like she'd seen a ghost.

Detective Howard sat next to her, slapping his notebook against his thigh.

Mom stood and filled a coffee cup three quarters full of milk, then added coffee and put it in front of me.

She handed me a sugar bowl and spoon.

"Detective Howard wants to talk to you." Her voice sounded sad.

I spooned sugar into the cup and stirred my milk coffee.

"Son, do you know who was shooting at the house?" Detective Howard asked.

"No," I said, and sipped the sweet milk coffee.

"Did you see anyone?" Detective Howard asked.

"A black Chevrolet," I said. "It was chopped. I didn't see any faces."

"What if we had been there?" Mom could barely speak.

"I don't think the shooting was meant for you or your son, Mrs. Cahill, if that's what has you worried," Detective Howard said. "From the graffiti on the walls, it looks like rival gangs are trying to claim the house."

That seemed to make Mom feel better. But it couldn't make her feel great to know rival gangs were fighting over the house.

Detective Howard folded the notebook and gave a business card to Mom.

She was so nervous, she began chewing on the edge of the card.

"Try not to worry," Detective Howard said.

Then he stood and left.

"If there's no need to worry, then how come we moved in here with Mrs. Washington?" I asked.

Mom got a strange look on her face.

Mrs. Washington said, "I need the rent money, for one thing."

Mom held up her hand. Her hands were always red from cleaning hotel rooms even though she wore big yellow rubber gloves. "Without Jimmy's money from his job at the restaurant, we can't afford to live there," Mom said.

I felt really bad I had asked now.

Mom's work cleaning hotel rooms wasn't enough.

"You left for school this morning before I got back," Mom said. "I didn't have a chance to explain everything to you." Then she choked up. "What would have happened to you if you had gone home to the old house?"

I didn't bother to tell her that I had. Or how Gus had saved my life.

I sipped the sweet milk coffee instead.

I didn't mind moving. I liked Mrs. Washington. Good smells always came from her kitchen. The best part was now I had a dog.

Spider must have read my mind. He jumped on my lap. His bony feet poked me like someone jabbing me with the blunt end of a knife.

"Get down, Spider," I yelled.

Mrs. Washington gave me a pooper-scooper. "I guess this will be your job now, Tito."

She and Mom laughed. Mom laughed too loudly, like she was desperate to make herself happy again.

I stood on the back porch with the pooper-scooper and watched Mom.

Mom saw me watching her and gave me the smile I used to see her give Jimmy.

"Take Mina with you," she said.

Mina and I went outside. I could hear police radios crackle on the other side of the fence.

I cleaned the yard with the pooper-scooper. Spider danced around my feet with a ball in his mouth.

"Why aren't dogs neat like cats?" Mina asked, following me.

"I don't know."

"Why doesn't Spider clean himself?"

"I don't know."

"Why do dogs leave such a mess all over? Can't dogs pick one place?"

"It's nature, Mina."

"Oh," she said.

I guess neatness is important if you're going to be a princess.

I had other things on my mind.

"Listen, Mina," I said. "You can't keep wandering off now. Things could be dangerous."

"Don't say that," Mina said. "You're making Spider scared."

Then she ran inside to Mom.

I guess if you're going to be a princess, you want to live in a safe world, too.

Jimmy had made our world safe.

At least I thought he had.

10

Mrs. Washington's house doesn't look like it from the outside, but it has two bedrooms upstairs. The walls slant and the windows jut out on the roof.

Mrs. Washington gave one upstairs room to me and the one across the hall to Mina. The rooms smelled of mothballs and Lysol spray, but even that couldn't cover the old smells of heat and dust.

I opened the window and hoped Mom didn't see. She'd make me close it so I wouldn't catch a cold. I think she really just felt better with the windows locked.

Mom had put my clothes in two drawers and in the closet. She'd even tacked my G.I. Joe posters on the walls even though I'd outgrown them.

I had never had my own bedroom.

Then I noticed Jimmy's clothes were gone.

"Mom, where is Jimmy's stuff?"

"I'm going to give it to people who need it more," she said.

"There's no one in the world who needs it more than I do," I said.

She looked at me curiously as if she was going to cry. I didn't want her to cry. Not again. I knew Jimmy would be mad at me if she did.

Then she smiled and said, "You're right. Help me carry the boxes up to your room."

Mom and I each carried a box up to my new room. Mina carried a shoe box filled with track medals and shoelaces and a stop watch.

Later, Mina and I went through the boxes. Jimmy didn't have much. He never got all the things he wanted. Jimmy always said he wanted money so he could hear life sing. He thought money made life better.

I looked in the first box, stuffed with T-shirts and jeans, and wondered how money or things could make life better. Maybe in the end Jimmy knew his life was singing with the way he made everyone laugh. I hoped he did.

I slept in Jimmy's old Raiders T-shirt. Mina slept with his track medals clutched in her hands.

A princess needs treasures, I guess.

That night something woke me. I sat up in bed, listening.

Spider had his nose on the windowsill, whining as if something had scared him.

When I was little, I woke up in the night. Many times. Because I thought I heard Dad coming home. He left when Mina was born. He couldn't take living here. He said if he had to be poor, he'd rather be poor in Tennessee, where he didn't have to breathe smog all day long. Mom wouldn't go back to Tennessee with him. She had dreams about a new life here in Los Angeles. She didn't want Jimmy and me to grow up and work in the mines.

I wondered if she had told Dad about Jimmy or if she even knew where Dad lived now.

I don't think about Dad the way I used to.

I stared at the dark and wondered if I would forget Jimmy the same way.

I promised myself that I would think about Jimmy at least once a day for the rest of my life.

Spider whined again.

A car door slammed.

I crept out of bed and looked out the window.

The blue Oldsmobile was parked in front of our old house.

Spider licked my hand. I kept scratching him behind his ear, trying to keep him quiet.

Lamar and Ice Breaker Joe stood on the sidewalk. The guy in the baseball cap, the one who wore the bandanna across his face like a bandit, used a crowbar to break open the front door to my old house.

They went inside.

A fourth guy stayed at the car and looked up and down the street, watching.

I didn't know if I should call the police or wake Mom.

Before I could decide, they ran back outside.

They jumped in the car and drove away. I wondered what they'd been doing inside. The house was empty.

Spider seemed okay then and jumped on my bed. I spent the rest of the night with paws poking my back.

I didn't sleep much. I couldn't figure why they broke into the house. What were they looking for? How did Detective Howard know they weren't after me, or my mom or Mina?

I shivered.

It wasn't cold air from the open window that made me shiver.

I was afraid.

11

When I woke up the next morning, sunlight hit my face. I had forgotten how happy early-morning sunshine made me feel. In my old room, boards covered the broken window.

Spider was barking in the backyard. He must have thought he was a rooster.

I jumped out of bed and pulled on my jeans. I took one of Jimmy's T-shirts from the box. The shirt hung down to my knees. I liked the style. Mom wouldn't let me buy shirts that big, but I didn't think she'd tell me I couldn't wear Jimmy's.

Mina was dressed for kindergarten. She sat in front of the TV, eating Rice Krispies with too much sugar and watching Nickelodeon.

I warmed milk and poured it over buttered toast. I like milk toast better than cereal.

Mom had already left for work.

I ate milk toast and watched Mrs. Washington peel apples at the sink. I hoped that meant she was baking an apple pie. She sang while she worked. Her voice was rich and thick, and I didn't want to stop her song with my stupid questions about pie.

When Mina and I went outside to walk to school, Zev waved from his front yard.

He carried his books in a small suitcase. He wore a black jacket and a white shirt tucked in. His black shoes shone. How was he ever going to make friends when his mom made him dress like an old man?

I tossed my backpack over my shoulder.

"Hi, Tito," Zev said. "Do you want to play after school?"

"I can't today," I lied.

Zev went to another school across town. His mom thought our school was too violent. The first week after his family arrived in the United States, his mother paid me a dollar to ride the Metro with Zev so he wouldn't get lost. He had to wear a little cap all the time. Mom told me it was a yarmulke, and that he wore it because he was

Jewish. I thought he'd get into fights over it, but no one seemed to mind at his school.

Mina and I waved good-bye and started off. I liked the sound Jimmy's tennis shoes made on the sidewalk.

When we were halfway to school, Mina asked, "Where do dragons live?"

"Where did you hear about dragons?" I asked, trying to think of an answer.

"On TV. A knight has to slay a dragon for me."

"Do you know what slay means, Mina?"

She looked at me in a way that meant she didn't.

"It means kill," I said.

She thought for a minute. "I'll ask my knight to put the dragon in a zoo then."

"Good," I said. "Dragons live on Komodo Island."

She looked at me to see if I was teasing.

The Komodo dragon isn't really a dragon, just a large lizard. A lizard ten feet long that weighs three hundred pounds and has clawed feet and a forked tongue is close enough, so I wasn't really lying.

When we got to Big Molly's Diner, I saw the front end of a blue Oldsmobile parked at the side of the building. I was sure it was the same car I saw last night. I wanted to find out who the other guy was, the one who wore the bandanna tied across his face.

"Mina, wait here. I'm going inside. I'll only be a minute. Promise me you won't go anywhere."

She nodded and leaned against a brick planter.

I went inside. Ice Breaker Joe and Lamar sat in a booth, stuffing Big Molly's special scrambled eggs, made with onions and hot green chili peppers, into their mouths.

I took a step closer to see if there was anyone else in the booth with them.

That's when I felt someone tug on my shirt. I turned around. Mina stood behind me.

"Mina, I told you to wait outside," I whispered.

"I got scared about dragons," Mina said.

Mina stared at a plate of French fries soaking in country gravy. The man seated at the counter eating the fries put his newspaper between Mina and his breakfast as if he thought Mina was going to steal his precious fries.

I took her hand. We went to the telephone near the bathrooms. I punched 911. I wasn't even sure what I was going to say. I couldn't say these guys broke into an empty house last night. Did that sound like a crime, with everything else that was happening?

I was ready to hang up when Lamar saw me.

He looked directly at me. He stood and walked toward me, his eyes half closed, trying to scare me.

It worked.

Ice Breaker Joe followed him.

I dropped the phone receiver.

"Go on to school, Mina," I whispered.

She's always wandering away, but now when she should have run, she stayed next to me. She must have thought she was watching Nickelodeon.

Lamar stood over me, big and tall and mean.

"How's Jimmy's business?" Lamar said with his onion-smelling breath.

"What do you mean?"

"I said how is Jimmy's business?"

Ice Breaker Joe laughed. His chipped teeth looked yellow and rotted.

"Run, Mina, run," I whispered.

She grabbed my shirt instead and twisted her hand in it.

I grabbed Mina's hand and dove into the women's rest room.

I thought going into the women's rest room would stop Lamar.

Lamar followed me in.

I've never heard a door bang so loudly against a wall.

12

Lamar stared at me.

"You and me, we got business," he said.

Then the door banged open again, hitting the same tile Lamar had broken seconds before.

Dust and pieces of tile fell to the floor.

Ice Breaker Joe jumped into the rest room, grabbed Lamar's arm, and jerked him out.

Sirens broke the morning air.

I had forgotten that when you dial 911 and leave the phone off the hook, computers give the location to the police department.

Tires squealed outside.

Sirens grew louder, then more distant. I guessed the cops were chasing the blue Olds. I waited with Mina. I didn't know what to do.

Mina solved the problem.

"I have to go to the bathroom," she said.

"Now?" I asked. Dumb question. "Okay. I'll wait."

I figured if I left the women's rest room now, I'd be in trouble anyway.

Mina entered a stall, and I sat on the sink counter.

I began to think maybe I was imagining all kinds of things. Was it just an overactive imagination? Did Lamar really ask me about Jimmy's business? What did that mean?

What kind of business did he have with me?

Maybe the words didn't mean what I thought they meant. Gangbangers make up new meanings to words. That way no one but their own gang members can understand what they're talking about.

The door to the women's rest room opened.

I'd forgotten where I was. I jumped off the counter and was face to face with Lisa Tosca.

"Oh, excuse me," Lisa said and walked back out. She looked at the door and came back in.

"Hi," I said like this was perfectly normal. I had never planned on meeting her in the women's rest room in Big Molly's Diner.

How could my life get more messed up?

Mina flushed the toilet.

Lisa stared at me while I helped Mina wash her hands. Even with her mouth wide open, Lisa looked pretty.

"'Bye," I said; then we left.

When we got outside, I screamed with frustration.

Mina jumped.

I didn't mean to frighten her.

"Sorry, Mina," I said. How could I explain it to her?

One block from school, Gus jumped from an alley and grabbed my backpack.

"Give it back, Gus," I said.

"It's mine now," Gus said.

He teased me, holding my backpack away from me like he wanted me to chase him for it. He hadn't done something that stupid since first grade.

"Give me back my backpack," I said.

I wasn't going to chase him.

Finally he came back.

"Here," he said, and handed it to me.

I swung the backpack over my shoulder. It felt really heavy.

I unzipped it and looked inside.

A gun sat on top of the peanut-butter-and-pickle sandwiches I had made that morning.

"You know what to do with it," Gus said. "You got to get revenge for Jimmy."

My hands started shaking.

"Take it back," I said. "I don't want it."

"You'll need it when the guys in the black Chevy come looking for you again," Gus said. "It's a gift from me and my homies. With Jimmy gone, you need us. Use the gun to show us what you got."

I shook my head. I felt like my heart was pounding so fast that my lungs couldn't breathe. "I don't want it, Gus."

"You don't want people treating you like you're nothing. You need a family," Gus said. "Being in a gang, it's the flying-est feeling." Then he started running down the block.

I ran after him, but I was afraid to run too fast. What if the gun went off?

I lost him.

I zipped the backpack closed.

"What did Gus put in your bag?" Mina asked when she caught up with me.

She reached for my backpack.

I slapped her hand really hard.

She looked at me, shocked. I had never hit her. Ever. Not even when we were little.

She started to cry.

"I'm sorry, Mina." I didn't put my arms around her like I would have any other time.

I couldn't.

I was afraid the gun might go off. I had heard too many stories about kids shooting their friends because they didn't know how to handle a gun. I didn't know anything about guns.

Maybe I imagined it.

I unzipped the backpack and looked inside again. There it was, a big cold metal gun.

I zipped the backpack closed and looked for Mina. She'd run off. We were close to school. I hoped she'd gone on to her kindergarten class.

There was no way I was going to go looking for her now. I had big problems of my own.

Someone tapped my shoulder.

I screamed and turned around.

Lisa Tosca stood behind me.

"Why did you scream?" she asked.

"It's something guys do to get ready for football season," I lied, hoping she didn't have any brothers.

"Oh," she said.

Then she added, "I think it's sweet the way you take care of your sister."

She had a neat smile.

"Want to walk me to school?" she said.

Of course I wanted to walk her to school, but I kept thinking about the gun.

"Did you hear me?" she asked.

"Not today," I said.

She stopped smiling. She still looked pretty.

"Sorry," I said.

She started walking away like she couldn't get far enough from me.

"Tomorrow," I yelled after her. "Tomorrow I'll walk you to school. I promise."

I knew she thought I was nuts.

If anything more happened I *would* be nuts.

13

The day was bad.

First I thought I'd give the gun to the principal, but he wasn't going to be at school for another hour. He had a meeting at the district office. I said I'd wait, but as I sat in his office, I kept thinking how much trouble Gus was going to get into. Then I started worrying that the principal wouldn't believe me and I'd be the one in trouble.

Jimmy was right. I'm nothing but a worry toad.

Finally I left the principal's office and went to class.

"You're late," Mrs. Bilky said.

"Sorry," I said, and handed her my pass.

She looked at it, then put it in her roll book.

Gus gave me a really angry look when I got to class. I think he knew what I was doing. When I sat down, he took my backpack and lifted it. I guess he could tell by the weight that I still had the gun.

He smiled and turned back to Mrs. Bilky.

Mrs. Bilky stood in front of the class showing how light passes through prisms. Like we hadn't seen that a million times before.

She yelled at me twice for not paying attention.

Later she came by my desk. She apologized and told me she was giving me a referral to a grief counselor.

Some days I go home for lunch, but other days I stay at school so I can work on the computers. On those days I eat lunch at school. Today was my day to work on the computers, but I couldn't eat the sandwiches I had packed. I didn't want to take any chances pulling out my sandwiches and having the gun go off.

My stomach grumbled all afternoon.

Kids in the front rows turned around and gave me funny looks.

Finally, Gus handed me some sunflower seeds. It's really hard to eat sunflower seeds in Mrs. Bilky's class, but I did that day.

When I got home, the house smelled like freshly baked apple pie.

"Do you want a piece of apple pie?" Mrs. Washington asked.

"Yes, please," I shouted.

I went upstairs. I took the gun from my backpack and hid it in the bottom of one of Jimmy's boxes; then I shoved the box under the bed and placed the other box in front of that. I hoped Mom didn't decide she had to go through Jimmy's things again.

Then I remembered Detective Howard gave me his card. I had it someplace. I found it in my drawer. I could tell Detective Howard about the gun. I'd tell him I found it in the alley.

I ran downstairs. I was about to pick up the phone when I saw Mina on Mrs. Washington's lap.

She was crying.

"What's wrong with Mina?" I asked. I thought she was still upset with me.

"Spider ran away because we're too sad," Mina said. "No one pays any attention to him, and he's lonely and misses Jimmy."

"He must have jumped the fence in the backyard," Mrs. Washington said.

"I'll help you find Spider," I said.

"What about your pie?" Mrs. Washington asked.

"I'll eat it when I get back," I said.

My stomach growled in protest.

I crammed one bite into my mouth. Mina headed for the door.

Mina and I walked up and down the streets. We asked everyone we saw if they had seen a dog that looked like a spider. People laughed until they looked at Mina. Then they got serious and tried to help.

"We're going to have to go back, Mina," I said. "It's getting late."

"One more block," Mina said. "Please."

"Okay," I said.

We turned down a side street and then another. Then we were lost.

Now I know how Mina feels when she wanders off and gets lost and why she's always crying when I find her.

Nighttime was no time to be on the street.

Mina and I walked to the corner. I looked both ways down the street. Traffic crossed at an intersection several blocks away. We walked down there; then I looked both ways again, trying to find a street with more traffic than this one. I knew if I kept following traffic, sooner or later I would find a street I knew.

I tried to cheer up Mina.

"Spider is probably home by now," I said. "I bet he's barking and wondering where you are. I hope he doesn't jump the fence again and go looking for you."

She smiled then.

The moon had risen, huge and ivory yellow, by the time we got home.

The backyard was empty. I could feel how disappointed Mina was. I walked up the back steps feeling defeated.

Mom was talking quietly to Mrs. Washington.

"Those boys just came in the backyard and took Spider," Mrs. Washington said.

"Don't tell the kids," Mom said.

I knew something bad had happened to Spider then, but I didn't want Mina to know. She was still in the backyard thinking Spider would come out and play with the Frisbee she held in her hand.

We ate dinner in silence, me knowing their secret.

They weren't the only ones with a secret.

I kept thinking about the gun and what I was

going to say to Detective Howard so he would think I found the gun in the alley.

That night I couldn't sleep. I was in bed, staring at the ceiling and watching the way car lights push shadows across the ceiling.

I guess Mom figured I was asleep, because her crying started again.

When Mom stopped crying, the house was quiet for a long time.

I was drifting off to sleep when I heard footsteps in the hallway.

Someone stood in my doorway.

"Tito."

I nearly fell out of bed.

"Mina, why are you up?" I said.

"I hear noises in the backyard," Mina said. "Go see if Spider's back."

"You stay here. I don't want you catching a cold on top of everything else."

I tucked her into my bed, pulled on my jeans, and carried Jimmy's sneakers downstairs, then put them on.

The moon colored the backyard an odd icy gray. Shadows looked like huge monsters crouching against the garage and house. It felt too silent outside, as if everyone had disappeared and I was alone in the world.

I started across the lawn to the doghouse when I heard footsteps coming across the wet grass behind me.

14

I turned.

Gus stood behind me holding a can of spray paint. He smiled.

I was still angry with him about the gun.

I glanced at Mrs. Washington's house, ready to fight if I saw any graffiti on the weathered stucco.

"Relax, man," Gus said, like he knew what I was thinking. "I came over to see if you wanted to join our tagging party."

"I already told you I'm not joining any gang."

Only a summer back we'd camped out in the backyard in a stupid tent we made with blankets. Now he was going one way and I was going another, and it was like we both knew it but didn't want to say it, so we just stood there in the backyard, knowing this was it.

"I want you to take your gun back, Gus," I said finally. "Wait here while I go get it."

"How 'bout just hanging out with me?" Gus said. "Then afterward I'll take the gun back."

I thought for a second. "If you don't do any tagging," I said.

He nodded.

I did like to spend time with Gus. There was a time when I thought we'd be best friends for life.

"I'll buy you a hamburger," Gus said.

"You know a place open now?"

"Big Molly's Diner," Gus said. "Come on."

"Are you sure it's open?" I asked.

"Would you stop worrying so much?" Gus said. "If it's closed, we'll go someplace else."

He started running down the alley. I tied Jimmy's shoes tighter and ran after him.

Our footsteps echoed down the empty streets.

Every time I got close enough to run with him, he'd sprint ahead of me.

Finally he turned into the parking lot of Big Molly's Diner.

I caught up to him. The diner was dark.

Gus looked at me, punched at my hand, and whispered, "Sorry."

I turned.

There was Spider, tied to the bumper of the blue Oldsmobile.

Lamar and Ice Breaker Joe leaned against the car hood.

I still didn't recognize the guy sitting in the driver's seat, but it hit me now who the other guy had been, the one with the baseball cap and bandanna over his face like a bandit.

I've never hated anyone as much as I hated Gus right then.

Ice Breaker Joe untied Spider.

"We found your doggie," Lamar said.

Spider ran to me. He jumped up, his stick legs poking me, and licked my face. Then he stopped and cringed next to my feet, whining.

I guess he sensed my fear.

15

"Just chill," Lamar said. "Jimmy was our friend."

"He wasn't a gangbanger," I said.

They laughed, even Gus.

"Jimmy was my ace man," Lamar said. "He didn't deserve what happened to him. Now people out looking for *you*. You need us to protect you so they won't mess with you. You don't want what happened to Jimmy to happen to you."

"I can handle my own," I said.

"Not against another gang," Lamar said. "You need the protection of your own family."

"I respect you," I said. Jimmy told me all gangbanging was about getting respect. I hoped I was showing enough to Lamar. "But I have to support my mother and sister."

They laughed again.

"How do you think Jimmy was supporting you all?" Lamar said. "Running drugs for me. That's how he did it. You join up with me, I can give you a good life, too."

"No, Jimmy wouldn't," I said.

"Jimmy did," Lamar said. "There's something Jimmy owed me that's still missing. I want you to find it."

"Uh-huh," I said. What was I going to say, no? I didn't want to get killed right there.

Lamar kept talking, and I kept giving Gus looks like death rays. I couldn't believe a friend could do this to me.

I guess I was wrong.

He's not my friend.

Gangbangers don't really have friends, even though they call each other family.

I took a step back and saw the back of the car.

Red cloth, held with electrical tape, covered the taillight closest to me. I remembered the taillights the night Jimmy was shot. Different colors. One red, one orange. Blurring as the car disappeared into the night.

The truth hit me like a bullet. They had killed Jimmy. Not someone in the black Chevy like Gus and Lamar wanted me to believe. Why would they kill Jimmy if he was their ace man? Why did they want me to think a rival gang killed Jimmy? Did they want me to think it was the guys in the black Chevy, just so I'd join up with them? That was crazy. Except if what Jimmy had was really important and they needed me to find it for them. But what could Jimmy have had that I wouldn't know about? I couldn't stop staring at those taillights.

Lamar put his heavy hand on my neck and squeezed. "What you looking at?"

16

"I was thinking about Jimmy," I said. "What did Jimmy owe you?"

His hand dropped away.

"Go home to your momma, baby boy," Lamar said. "If you don't know what Jimmy owed me, then you're dumber than you look."

He made some motion with his hand, and they all got into the car, Gus included.

Gus stepped around me like I wasn't there anymore.

The car pulled away, and only then did I realize how scared I had been. My palms were wet and I could feel my heart beating in my head.

At home I took Spider into the house. Mina was asleep on the floor under my window. I carried her back to her bed.

Spider jumped up, circled twice, and curled

next to Mina, resting his head against her.

I crawled into my bed, but I knew I wasn't going to sleep.

They said they weren't the ones who killed Jimmy. They lied to me, so how could I trust anything they said? Even Gus lied to me. Did Jimmy really sell drugs?

I didn't think he could have. Jimmy told me it was hopeless if you joined a gang. Rivals did drive-by shootings at your house, and you always lived in fear.

The next day after school, I rode the Metro downtown with Mom. She was going to get Jimmy's last paycheck. She went into the restaurant and came out with an odd look on her face.

"The man said Jimmy never worked here."

"Maybe he forgot," I said.

"I asked the other busboys," she said. "No one knew him."

"Maybe Jimmy did belong to a gang," I said.

But she didn't want to hear it.

"I went to the wrong restaurant," Mom said. "I don't know this city very well."

"You're right, Mom," I said. "It's probably another restaurant where Jimmy worked."

I agreed with her even though I didn't believe it anymore. I didn't see why I should ruin Mom's memory of Jimmy.

I leaned back and rested my head next to the window as the Metro banged over the rails. I'd have to figure out something on my own if my family was going to have any kind of future.

I thought about the gun again. There had to be another way. Lamar was right about one thing. I didn't want to end up like Jimmy.

I opened my eyes and looked at Mom. She was staring straight ahead. She didn't need another funeral either.

When we got home, Mom and Mrs. Washington cooked dinner. Mrs. Washington made a carrot salad, and Mom scrambled cheese into eggs and made hot biscuits filled with sliced bananas and topped with mayonnaise.

I ate too much and then got mad at myself for thinking about food when there was so much else going on.

I sat on my bed wearing Jimmy's baseball glove and throwing his baseball into the pocket.

Maybe I could give those gangbangers exactly what they wanted.

I took my shower and got ready for bed. I didn't want to fall asleep, but it was really hard not to.

I woke up hours later. I dressed, put on Jimmy's shoes, and searched in the boxes for Jimmy's flashlight. Then I went outside and climbed the fence into my old backyard.

Jimmy had told me about a crawl space under the house once.

I moved a board behind the pink hibiscus bush and shone the flashlight into the space under the house.

Spiderwebs and rusted pipes filled the gloom. There was room to move inside and crawl around.

I knew if Jimmy had hidden anything, this was the only place he could have hidden it from Mom. She was always vacuuming under beds and moving mattresses and cleaning our closets.

I crawled in. Spiderwebs covered my face. I held my breath and spit, then brushed the webs away. It smelled wet and gross under the house.

I crawled on my belly about three feet; then I heard a car pull up outside.

Car doors opened.

I turned off the flashlight. It was pitch-black under the house.

I didn't have enough time to go back to Mrs. Washington's house. I stayed there and hoped the gangbangers, if they were gangbangers, didn't know about the crawl space.

Soon I heard footsteps on the floor above me, then loud creaking noises as if they were prying wallboards away with crowbars. Maybe they thought Jimmy had hidden whatever it was in the walls.

I waited for what seemed like hours.

Finally footsteps pounded toward the front door. The house got quiet. Car doors opened and closed. A car pulled away. Silence followed.

I waited five minutes before I turned on my flashlight.

In the beam of light I saw a suitcase. I crawled over and opened it. Stacks of money filled the suitcase.

There was a note to me on top.

Tito,

Well little brother, if you're reading this, I guess you've been to my funeral.

Probably my homies found out I was skimming cash and laid me down, but who knows? I didn't lie when I told you gangsters are either dead or going to be.

Banging was fun at first when I was kicking back with my homies. But then it seemed like all we did was go to funerals and cause more. I thought if I could get enough money, I could take you and Mina and Mom someplace safe. Sorry I didn't get you there.

But you can get there, Tito. Be strong. Use the money. Make your life sing.

Jimmy

I couldn't help it. I started crying. I cried really hard for Jimmy.

I took the note and closed the suitcase.

I crawled back outside, feeling dusty and covered with spiders. I started to walk back to the house when I heard someone behind me.

Before I could turn, someone knocked me to the ground.

17

Zev was on top of me.

"Sorry, Tito," Zev said. "I didn't mean to knock you over. I tripped."

"What are you doing here? Don't you have rules about this kind of thing?" His mother had a rule about everything.

"I thought you might be in trouble."

"How did you know I was here?"

"I can see from my bedroom window. I was watching all the time in case the gangbangers captured you. I was going to call 911. When you didn't come out, I was afraid you were trapped."

I looked at him and shook my head. The kid knew nothing about sneaking out at night. He still had his pajamas on. How was he going to explain grass stains on his pj's to his mom?

"Thanks," I said finally, and wrapped my arm over his shoulder.

"Zev," I said, "am I your first friend since you've come to America?"

He laughed and it sounded fake. "I have a million friends," he said.

"Good," I said. "Because right now you don't want to get caught hanging out with me."

I climbed back over the fence and left him standing in the backyard. I figured he had enough sense to go home.

In my bedroom I took the gun from its hiding place and put it in my backpack between my science book and my English book.

Tomorrow was going to be a big day for me.

18

I got up early and left the house with the backpack over my shoulder.

I didn't eat breakfast. Skipping a meal upsets Mom. That was nothing compared to what she was going to do when she found out I didn't wait to walk Mina to school.

I couldn't worry about eating or being in trouble with Mom with everything else that was going on.

A trash truck whined and coughed down the alley. I ran after it. When the men weren't looking, I flung my backpack over the top into the bin. I stood next to the poinsettia and waited, hoping the gun wouldn't fire.

Motors whined. The big truck began compressing the trash.

Then I ran to Big Molly's Diner.

Lamar and Ice Breaker Joe stood outside, holding cartons filled with French fries. Steam rose from the chili covering the fries.

I walked up to them, pretending not to be afraid. They laughed at me, but I kept thinking what Mom always said about whoever laughs last, laughs best.

"I figure I know where Jimmy left the stuff he owes you if there ever was any stuff," I said. I wasn't going to tell them I had seen it.

"Look how tough he's acting now," Ice Breaker Joe said.

"Jimmy crawled under the house all the time saying he was fixing pipes," I said.

They looked at each other. Something connected in their big dumb brains.

"There's a board over the entrance to the crawl space behind the pink hibiscus plant. You'd never see it if you didn't know it was there. But I wouldn't go there," I said.

"And why wouldn't you go there?" Lamar asked, and stuffed a mess of French fries covered with chili and cheese in his mouth.

"Because cops have been watching the house day and night."

"There's no cops there unless they're invisible," Ice Breaker Joe said.

"Yeah, well, I guess they're all undercover," I said. "I see them all the time."

"Then why don't you go get the stuff?" Lamar said.

"Because I'm no gangbanger and neither was Jimmy."

"Then why you telling us about under the house?" Lamar said.

"I did what you asked so all the gangbangers would stop coming around and breaking into the house. I told you. I warned you. Now we're even." I started walking away. I walked really slow even though my legs were hammering with nerves.

I walked into Big Molly's Diner and took a seat.

Sonny came over. "Those boys at the car bothering you?"

I shook my head so Lamar and Ice Breaker Joe could see and know I wasn't a squealer.

Sonny placed a menu on the counter and gave me a glass of water.

When I heard the car pull away, I went to the pay phone and punched in 911.

The only undercover cop who had been hanging around the house was me.

I told the voice on the line that Jimmy Cahill had hidden drug money he stole from his gang under the house at 1501 Logan Street, and that the gangbangers who killed him were going to get it now. Then I hung up.

I knew police would be buzzing around here and buzzing around the house, so I went up to Sonny.

"My mom gave me money for breakfast and I lost it," I lied. I'd been telling too many lies. I promised myself this was my last. "I tried to call and no one's home. Do you have any work I can do to earn money for breakfast?"

Sonny gave me a doubtful look. He didn't know if I was gaming him or not.

"You want to clean the rest rooms?" he asked.

I nodded.

"I'll give you breakfast every morning," he said, "if you'll clean out the rest rooms every day. I hate that job."

"Can I bring my sister sometimes?"

"How old is she?"

"She just turned five," I said. "She likes French fries."

"All right."

By the time I was rolling the bucket of suds into the bathroom, I heard sirens. I was glad to be hiding out in the bathroom with Clorox fumes in my nose. That way I had an excuse to mind my own business and I didn't have to get in anyone's way.

I finished and went back to Sonny.

He checked into the men's rest room, then knocked on the women's door and, when no one answered, ushered me inside.

"Good job, son," he said when I finished. "You've got a job."

He held out his hand for me to shake.

"Call me Sonny," he said. "Everyone does."

I shook his hand. He was a nice man. I wondered if he was married. He looked so skinny, I knew he could use Mom's cooking.

"What do you want to eat?" he asked.

"Could I wait until lunch and come back with my sister? She'll be really impressed if I can treat her to some French fries."

He chuckled, but his laugh felt good.

"You bet," he said.

Gus didn't show up at school.

I sat in my classroom all morning, really nervous.

I wondered what had happened, but I knew not to ask anyone because that would be too suspicious. I had to wait and let the news come to me.

Mrs. Bilky busted me for losing my science book and my English book. She asked Lisa to share her books with me and said we should do our science and English together until I found my books.

At lunchtime, I picked up Mina from kindergarten and we walked home.

Yellow police tape was flapping all around the front yard of our old house. They had cut down the pink hibiscus bush in the side yard.

Mina and I went inside Mrs. Washington's house.

Mom and Mrs. Washington stood at the window, looking outside. Mom wore her white uniform. Someone had gone to the hotel where she worked and brought her home.

"They caught Jimmy's killers," Mom said. "At least they think they have. Detective Howard said they have a gun that they think will match the bullets found in Jimmy." Mom's words choked then.

I just nodded.

"Why did you leave this morning without breakfast or Mina?" Mom asked. She fisted her hands on her hips. That meant she was serious.

I looked out the window.

"I had to finish some work for Jimmy. It's what he would have wanted me to do."

She took in air in a huge gasp and hugged me so tight, I couldn't breathe.

"Mom," I said.

"No more," she said. "No more."

She let me go then.

"I'm going to take Mina down to Big Molly's Diner for French fries," I said.

"How did you get money?" She looked scared.

"Don't worry, Mom," I said. "I scrubbed out the bathrooms. You can call Sonny and check. You don't have to worry about me. Sonny gave me a job scrubbing out the bathrooms so Mina and I can have French fries every day."

"For me?" Mina said. She was so happy, she did look like a princess then.

Big Molly's Diner was really busy. Mina and I sat at the counter. Mina spread a paper napkin over her lap and tucked another one into her collar.

I liked playing big brother to Mina the way Jimmy used to do.

Behind us a woman was passing out paper

party hats, crowns and pirate hats and pointed caps. She had one gold crown left over.

I saw Mina stare at it, then turn around and dunk her French fry in gravy and slip it in her mouth.

"I'm going to the bathroom," I said, but then I went over and asked the woman if I could buy the crown for my baby sister.

I didn't have any money. I was hoping the woman would give me the party hat. I mean, what kind of person would sell a kid a paper party hat that would end up in the trash anyway?

"I have extra," the woman said. "You can have it."

"Thank you," I said.

I handed the gold-paper crown to Mina.

Mina nearly swallowed her French fry whole.

She wiped her fingers on her napkin and put the crown on her head.

I sat there feeling my toes stretch to the end of Jimmy's shoes.

I wanted Mina's life to be perfect. I never wanted her to grow up needing a gang. Maybe she *can* become a princess, or at least play a princess in the movies, if she keeps her mind on her goal.

How could Jimmy ever join a gang? Maybe he

had too much responsibility helping Mom, but in the end I knew that in his heart he wasn't a gang-banger. Jimmy liked life too much.

After dinner that evening, I picked up my baseball and glove and Jimmy's, too. I walked across the street and knocked on Zev's door.

Zev opened the door.

"Can you come outside?" I asked. "I want to show you how to play baseball."

I've never seen a guy smile as big as Zev did that day.

I did learn how to play chess, and then I taught Lisa. She's good at it and always beats me.

I'm sure Jimmy's laughing about that. He's probably laughing at all the crazy singing my life does.

At least I hope he is.